D1562989

TOMBSTONE JACK AND THE REDWING SALOON

Also by Dan Winchester

Tombstone Jack
Tombstone Jack and the Redwing Saloon

TOMBSTONE JACK AND THE REDWING SALOON

Dan Winchester

Denton & White
2017

Tombstone Jack and the Redwing Saloon
© 2017 by Gary Jonas

Any similarity to anyone living or dead is a figment of your overactive imagination, so don't go there. The author made it all up, okay? No ifs ands or buts about it.

This edition published by Denton & White

April 2017

ISBN-13: 978-1545289259
ISBN-10: 1545289255

This one is for Gordon, who didn't live long enough to read it.

CHAPTER ONE

Jack Coltrane knew they were being followed. A cold wind howled down the streets of the Barbary Coast in San Francisco, carrying the smell of desperation. The roads were muddy from the previous night's rain, and the sun had only begun to shoot rays of orange light across the clouds. Shadows stretched, and a rooster crowed in the distance.

Jack and Burt were on foot. They'd left their horses in the care of a livery stable when they'd arrived in town the night before. Nobody had been following them at that time.

They checked into a hotel a short time later, and everything was fine.

This morning, however, it was another story. Three, maybe four men. Jack nudged Burt toward a side street beside a dance hall. "Let's go this way," Jack said.

"I thought we was meeting your friend at the Cobweb Palace." Burt kept his hand on his hat to keep it in place as they walked. The hat was two sizes too big and always seemed to be falling off his head, but he refused to buy a new one.

"We will, but we have a gang of cut-throats on our trail."

"Say what?" Burt's eyes grew wide as saucers. He was a slight man with a scraggly beard, and while he'd gained some measure of confidence riding from Texas to California with Jack, he was still a bit skittish.

Jack, on the other hand, was a large, powerful man clad in a duster that made him seem even bigger. Not only was he tall, but he made his living going after the baddest of the bad.

"Slow down a bit," Jack said. "I don't want to lose them."

"Don't want to lose them? Are you crazy?"

Jack grinned. "We'll slip into that alley over there." He nodded toward a narrow, dark gap between two buildings. "That's where they'll strike."

"I don't want to be trapped in an alley with them."

"You're getting it wrong, Burt. They'll be trapped in an alley with me."

"Shouldn't you at least open up that coat so you can get to your gun?"

"They won't shoot us," Jack said. "These are knife guys."

"You ain't helping to put me at ease, Jack."

"Knives can be more dangerous than guns. When we get into the alley, I want you to find a place to hunker down out of sight."

"Hide?"

"That's right."

"First sensible thing you've said to me all morning. What about you?"

"I'll have a little chat with the gang."

"All by your lonesome?"

"Do you want me to save one for you?"

"Hell no."

"Then I'll handle it. You just be quiet."

"I'll try to keep my whimpering down. Why can't we just move faster and avoid these guys?"

Jack pushed Burt down the alley. A stack of broken wooden crates had been toppled over and blocked the opposite end. A man lay face-down on the ground about halfway down the passage. "They'll prey on someone else."

"Sounds good to me."

"I don't want them to prey on anyone."

"So you're gonna get yourself killed before we even talk to your friend."

"Go stretch out by that guy over there," Jack said and pointed to the man in the center.

Burt hurried ahead, and when he reached the body, he saw stab wounds in the back. He started to tell Jack, but someone kicked a few boxes out of the way, so Burt dropped to the ground and tried to be still.

Two men strolled past Burt. One held a large knife and the other carried a baseball bat. Burt held his breath as they closed in on Jack.

Two more men entered the mouth of the alley, trapping him. Both wielded knives, though one also had a gun in a holster tied off on his left leg. Jack thought of him as "Lefty."

Jack leaned against the wall of a building. The stench of rotting garbage filled the air. "Howdy, boys," Jack said.

"Hello yourself," Lefty said. "If you don't want any trouble, you just hand over all your cash and we'll let you live."

Jack laughed. "Who said I don't want trouble? I'd hate to lure you all the way down here for nothing."

"You ain't got no gun, asshole."

They kept moving toward him.

"As a matter of fact, I do," Jack said. "But I promise not to use it on you. To be honest, you're not worth the price of the bullets it would take to kill you."

"Big talk for someone whose buddy abandoned him."

"What makes you think he's not behind you to keep you from running away?" Jack asked.

One of the men turned to look.

"Money," Lefty said.

"Come and get it," Jack said.

"Edgar, Monte? Take his ass down."

Edgar and Monte were the two who passed Burt. They moved in. Edgar brandished the blade, but Monte came in first with the bat. Monte took a mighty swing at Jack's head.

At the same moment, Lefty and his friend raced forward.

Jack caught the bat with his right hand and stopped the swing. He pulled Monte off balance then spun and twisted the bat from the man's grip. He smacked Monte in the throat with the handle. Monte flopped backward to the ground. Jack spun the opposite way as Edgar tried to stab him. Jack continued the spin and swung the bat with all his strength. The bat cracked Edgar's skull open. Edgar was dead before he hit the ground.

Lefty tried to slash with his blade as his friend jumped back. Something about watching two men go down in less than a second took the confidence away and tossed it over to rot with the rest of the garbage.

"Let's get outta here!" the man said and took off running.

Jack threw the bat. It flipped end over end and struck the man in the back. The man fell face first into the mud and slid to a stop. Jack was disappointed because he'd been aiming for the man's head. Oh well.

Jack didn't have time to focus on him because Lefty slashed again. The blade cut through the sleeve of Jack's coat. Jack pulled back and the man hacked at him again. Facing a left-handed opponent felt backward, but Jack recovered quickly. He caught Lefty's knife hand, twisted hard, breaking the man's wrist. Jack snatched the blade from his loosened grip. Lefty howled in pain and tried to move back, but Jack stomped on his foot and shoved him. Lefty fell down and tried to scramble away, grabbed his pistol with his right hand. He had to flip it around in order to fire, but Jack didn't give him time. Jack threw the knife down into Lefty's chest with a soft *thunk*. He kicked the gun out of Lefty's hand before the man could squeeze the trigger.

"Play time is over, Burt," Jack said.

Burt climbed to his feet. His eyes went wide and he fumbled to draw his gun. He fired twice, three times.

Jack turned and watched the fourth man—the one who'd tried to run—stumble and fall to the ground. The knife in his hand bounced away.

"Nice shooting," Jack said.

"I missed twice."

"Third shot got him in the head."

"I was aiming for the chest."

"Either way, you did great. Thank you."

Burt puffed out his chest a bit and nodded. "Saved you, didn't I?"

Jack, who had heard the man coming, and was ready to turn around to handle him, nodded. "Indeed you did."

"This other guy's dead." Burt nodded to the corpse in the center of the alley.

"From what I understand, that's common out here."

"Why did we come here again?"

"Now, Burt, you can't feel alive until you've stared death in the eyes without blinking."

Burt shook his head. "You got some crazy notions about what it takes to feel alive. Me? I feel just fine in the arms of one of Madame Chauncey's girls."

"You have to pay for them."

Burt grinned. "Don't matter," he said. "It's worth every penny."

CHAPTER TWO

The Cobweb Palace had seen better days. The entrance was at the corner of the two story building, and several large windows faced the road, but they were so filthy, it was impossible to see inside the place.

Jack and Burt moved around an old man who slept in a chair leaning against the building. They went up the steps and pushed into the saloon. The rafters were covered in spider webs so thick they draped from the rafters looking like clouds.

"This place is creepy," Burt said.

Wooden masks from Africa leaned against one wall. Paintings adorned another wall, but with all the spider webs spun from frame to frame, it was impossible to determine the subjects. Three monkeys darted across an empty table, and a kangaroo bent over a water dish in the corner.

A lone couple occupied a table toward the back, and a gaunt man wearing a black top hat stood behind the bar talking to Jack's friend, an old woman named Mabel. Her husband, a dwarf named Tuck sat on a stool with his legs swinging back and forth as he sipped a drink. He shelled peanuts and rolled the nuts across the counter to a parrot.

"I don't want any spiders on me," Burt said staring at the webs. "My head itches. That better be a regular itch and not one of them creepy-crawlies."

"There aren't any spiders on you," Jack said. "Let's go talk to my friend."

Burt stopped and pointed. "Is that a bear?"

Jack ignored him and walked to the bar. "Howdy, Abe," Jack said to the man in the top hat and placed a few coins on the counter. "Two hot toddies, please."

"Good to see you again, Mr. Coltrane."

"Good to see you too. It's been a few years."

The woman leaned close to Jack. She sniffed him once, then took hold of his hand and turned it so she could get a better look. "You haven't changed your ways, Jack. You've been riding for days, and fighting this morning."

"I got here as fast as I could, Mabel." Jack turned and gestured to Burt. "This is my friend, Burt Nesterman. Burt, this is Mabel Townsend, and the gentleman beside her is her husband, Tuck."

Tuck didn't acknowledge them. He clucked at the parrot and gave it another peanut.

The parrot cussed.

"Dang bird," Burt said. "Don't it know there's a lady present?"

Mabel laughed. "My ears have suffered through far worse." Her eyes sparkled and her crow's feet deepened, but her eyes retained a haunted look.

Abe returned with two drinks. He set them down and gave Jack a nod. "I wasn't planning to open this early, but Chester and Gertie were hungry, so I invited them in. If you'll excuse me." He moved away to go take care of the couple at the back table.

A spider crawled up the bar. Burt made a fist and moved toward it, but Jack put a hand on his arm. "Abe likes his spiders," he said. "Don't kill it."

"That's just weird."

"I got you a hot toddy," Jack said and handed him a cup.

"What's that?"

"Whisky and gin boiled with cloves."

Burt sipped it. "That's pretty good."

Jack turned to Mabel. "Your telegram said you had a problem involving some wanted men and you needed help. Can you be specific now that I'm here?"

"The problem is with my son. Nathan's disappeared."

Jack bowed his head. "Any idea what happened?"

"Lawrence Morton happened."

"Lawrence Morton? That name sounds familiar."

"Scary Larry."

Jack nodded. "I haven't thought about him since I was boy."

"He and Nathan remained friends after you moved away."

Jack and Nathan had been boyhood friends back in Missouri; right up until Jack's father killed Jack's brother and mother, and then committed suicide. Jack had lived with Mabel and Tuck for six years before his Aunt Stella and

Uncle Gene agreed to take him to stay with them in the Kansas Territory.

Before Jack moved away, he and Nathan sometimes ran around with a kid named Larry. Everyone called him Scary Larry because he liked to hurt people and animals. He was the kid who would pull the wings off a butterfly to upset the girls at the schoolhouse.

"I never liked him," Jack said. "Nathan always felt sorry for him."

"Yes, well, Nathan always had a soft spot for outcasts. In any case, Lawrence invited Nathan to visit him. Said he had a business proposition. Nathan was still in Missouri, but after his house burned down, and Nathan had one too many run-ins with the sheriff, he left Springfield and joined us out here, but things weren't right. Tuck warned Nathan to steer clear of Lawrence."

"Tuck spoke?" Jack asked, surprised.

She shook her head. "He wrote it down."

"He can't talk?" Burt asked.

"He chooses not to," Mabel said. "Lawrence won't talk to Tuck, and I can't go into his saloon. Can you talk to Lawrence? Find out what happened to Nathan?"

"I'm not sure what good it will do."

"You're technically a lawman, right?"

"Technically, but if there's no bounty on Lawrence, I can't do more than talk to him. Is there a bounty?"

"Yes, it's five hundred dollars. Nobody's even trying to collect it because he's well-protected."

"Nobody's that well-protected," Jack said.

"Jack, I want you to take him in for the reward, of course, and he has a couple of men working for him with bounties as well, but I don't want you to collect on them right away. I'll pay you to find out what Lawrence did to

Nathan. Did he kill him? I can't pay much because we don't have much, but I need to know what happened to my son."

"I won't take your money, Mabel. You're family. And I'd be happy to talk to Lawrence for you. I'll see what I can learn before I take him in. Which saloon?"

"He runs the Redwing over on Montgomery." She gave him a slight nod. "Tuck is tired. We've been up all night. My gout is acting up again. You can find us at this address." She handed him a piece of paper with an address printed in shaky cursive.

Jack glanced at it. He recognized it as the same address they'd had two years before. "Still haven't moved?"

"Someday."

Tuck hopped off the stool, tossed one last peanut to the parrot. He held out a hand. Jack bent down enough to clasp it. Tuck gave him a firm handshake and a nod, then reached into his pocket and pulled out a foolscap page on which he'd printed the words, *Thank you*. He turned and followed Mabel as she limped out of the saloon. Tuck kept a hand up to steady her just in case, but didn't actually touch her.

Jack watched them go and seeing how Tuck was there for her made him feel good. She didn't know he was ready to catch her, but she didn't need to worry. He would always have her back.

CHAPTER THREE

That night, as Jack and Burt approached the Redwing Saloon, two men carried a sailor out through the batwing doors and chucked him into the mud. The backsplash caught Burt's boots and pant legs.

"Damn it!" Burt said.

The two large men glared at Burt, but when they turned their eyes to Jack the glare went away. Jack had that effect.

The sailor picked himself up, brushed off his shirt, shook mud from his hands, turned and started back toward the saloon. The men put out their hands and shook their heads in unison.

"Don't even think it," one of the men said.

"But I didn't do nothing," the sailor said.

"Take it somewhere else. You want a look at what Betsy has under that skirt, you gotta pay."

"She was practically putting it on display. I was just helping."

"Get the hell out of here, Wayne."

"Excuse us," Burt said.

The men parted to allow Jack and Burt to enter the saloon, then they closed ranks to block Wayne.

The Redwing was packed with men. Tables lined the edges of a large dance floor where pretty dancing girls shook their goods to attract paying customers. Booths lined the walls, and the bar stood at the back of the joint. A large blonde woman stood at the end of the bar with a scarred bruiser of a man seated next to her. A network of pink scars crawled over his forehead with one long mark running down his left cheek. A history of brawls and knife fights were recorded there, and the fact that he still drew breath was a testament to his fighting prowess. He gazed out at the men crowding the tables and booths, and Jack knew the man was sizing each up and dismissing them in a heartbeat. No threats.

Until his eyes fastened on Jack.

The man leaned over and spoke to the woman. She stared at Jack and nodded.

Jack didn't recognize Lawrence, but it had been many years, and he hadn't seen him since they were eleven years old. If they'd passed in the street, they'd have been strangers regardless.

"That your old friend?" Burt asked.

"We weren't friends."

"Acquaintance then?"

"I don't know. Let's find out."

They moved through the crowd to get to the bar.

"What can I do you for, gents?" the blonde asked.

"I'm here to see Lawrence Morton," Jack said.

"And you are?" the woman asked.

"Jack Coltrane."

"From Springfield?" the man said and narrowed his gaze.

"One and the same."

"Small world. You don't look anything like the Jack I knew back then."

"Hard years, and I can say the same for you."

"Definitely some hard years packed in there." He gestured to the bar counter beside him. "Stand over here, Jack. I need to be able to keep an eye on the door."

Burt started to move, but Jack put out a hand and blocked him.

"I'm fine where I am. Burt is too. I understand you went into business with Nathan."

Lawrence shrugged and grinned. "Tried to, but he elected not to take me up on my offer."

"Mind if I ask what that offer was?"

Lawrence shrugged again, and Jack figured it was his go-to mannerism. "Nate was a friend. I won't be making that offer to you. No offense, Jack, but I never liked you much."

"I never liked you either," Jack said.

Lawrence laughed. "Still honest as the day is long. Who's your sidekick?"

"This is Burt."

"So you're running around with another runt of the litter. Replacement for ol' Leroy?"

"Burt's a good man."

"Oh, I'm sure he is. Leroy might be too for all I know." Lawrence turned to the blonde. "Jack here used to have this little colored kid who followed him everywhere. Leroy's pa was a free man, so Leroy was too, but lots of us liked to kick the stuffing out of him every week. Jack didn't cotton to that and stood up for him." He turned back to Jack. "Whatever happened to little Leroy?"

"He died in the war."

"Well, damn." Lawrence turned to the bartender. "Heath, we need four whiskeys on the double."

"Yes, sir," Heath said.

The bartender filled four glasses and slid them down the bar.

Lawrence handed a glass each to the blonde, Jack, and Burt. He lifted his own glass. "To Leroy," he said, and once again gestured for Jack to move over to the bar.

Jack ignored the gesture. Everyone slammed the whiskey and set the glasses on the bar.

"I gotta admit that always kinda liked Leroy," Lawrence said, running a finger over the rim of his glass. "The word 'quit' was not in his vocabulary. Knock him down, he'd get right back up. And he knew better than to hit back on account of it would get him killed. He knew his place. Why, even after my daddy killed his daddy, he never fought back."

Jack didn't let anything show on his face. Burt looked from Lawrence to Jack and back again, and followed Jack's lead.

"So when was Nathan here?" Jack asked.

"Few weeks back, I guess. Right, Penny?"

The blonde nodded. "Sounds about right."

"Any idea where he went?"

"He didn't say."

"What was the business venture?"

Lawrence rubbed his chin and leaned to the side to look around Jack for a moment. "I wanted him to help manage the place, but he said it wasn't the kind of thing he wanted to do. I was a mite disappointed, truth be told, but I filled the position with someone else. Ain't seen ol' Nate since then, but if you happen see him, tell him to come on in and have a drink. Far as I'm concerned, we're friends till the day we die."

"And if you see him, can you tell him I'm looking for him?"

"For old time's sake, I'll do that for you, Jack. And if you want to stop by here, you're welcome anytime. Might even give you a discount on one of the dancing girls. Step over here and take a gander at the quality I got working tonight."

"I'm fine. Any clue where Nathan was staying?"

"With his ma and that dwarf."

"Tuck."

"That's the one. I was trying to remember his name. Ain't that right, Penny?"

"It right sure is," she said.

"If you see Nate's ma, you tell her hello for me."

"I'll do that. One little problem, and maybe you can shed some light on the situation. Nathan hasn't been seen since he went to see you."

"That can't be right," Lawrence said. "He was fine when he left here. Ain't that right, Penny?"

"Fit as a fiddle."

"And then some."

Jack looked around the saloon. He noted at least six men watching the conversation. Two had moved into position where they could draw their guns and catch Jack and Burt in a crossfire. "Well, I appreciate you taking the time to talk to us, Larry."

"It's Lawrence now."

"I'll make a note."

Lawrence nodded. "And you come back and see us, you hear?"

"We're staying at the Hotel Chevalier," Jack said. "I'm in room 207."

"With your new friend?"

"He has his own room."

"Glad to hear it."

"If you think of anything else that might help me find Nathan, feel free to drop by anytime," Jack said.

Lawrence shook his head. "Told you what I can, but if I hear anything, at least I know where to find you. Feel free to stick around. Things start getting lively after nine o'clock or so."

"Another time," Jack said. He gave a nod to Lawrence, then tipped his hat to Penny. "Ma'am."

As they crossed the floor toward the exit, two pretty women wearing tiny red vests, and short skirts that left little to the imagination, glided over to them. A brunette ran her index finger along Jack's jawline.

"Hey, gorgeous, care for a dance?" she asked.

A redhead leaned close to Burt, letting her vest fall open enough that his eyes would be drawn to her chest. "Buy me a drink at the bar and I'll give you a ride you'll never forget."

"Another time, ladies," Jack said.

"But—" Burt said.

"We'll do anything you want," the brunette said.

"I'm sure you would," Jack said

He dragged Burt away from them, and Burt kept looking back.

"Little slices of heaven," Burt said.

"You can't afford their kind of heaven."

"I beg to differ. I have some money, and I've blown it on a lot worse things."

"That's not what I meant."

He and Burt walked out of the saloon. The sailor who'd been tossed out was nowhere in sight.

"Why you want to ruin my action?" Burt asked when they were outside.

"You should settle for a nice woman, Burt."

"I'll settle for any woman I can get. I ain't getting no younger, and that redhead was ready, willing, and able to please me."

"They'll please anyone with money."

"And once again, I have money."

Jack shook his head. "There are other women. What did you think of Lawrence?"

"He was weird," Burt said. "He seemed talkative and open, but he's damn sure hiding something."

"Of course he is."

"And you went and told him where we're sleeping."

"Don't worry about it."

"Easy for you to say. He's the kind of man who'll slit your throat while talking about the weather."

"Maybe."

"You think he had something to do with Nathan's disappearance?"

"Oh, I know he did. Only question I have now is whether Nathan is alive or dead. Once we figure that one out, I'll drag Lawrence out of the Redwing and collect my reward."

"He had a couple fellas watching us real close," Burt said holding up two fingers in a V.

"You noticed two?"

"Yep," Burt said, proud.

"I noticed six."

"You got eyes in the back of your head?"

"I just pay attention."

"Hell, I'm so broke, I can't afford to pay attention."

"I thought you had money for that redhead."

"I'm-a saving that money for her, and that's why I'm broke."

"Well, there you go," Jack said.

CHAPTER FOUR

Lawrence Morton watched Jack and Burt head toward the door. He raised a hand and pointed to two of his dancing girls. Once he caught their attention, he pointed at the oddly paired cowboys. The women nodded and moved to intercept them.

Penny leaned close. "Suspicion runs deep in the big man."

Lawrence nodded.

"He wouldn't budge when you tried to get him to move."

"He's smarter than he looks," Lawrence said. "And he's not taking the bait."

"Want me to send Rod and Kenneth over to kill him?"

"No need to kill him just yet. Jack Coltrane was always a tough kid, and I gotta admit I looked up to him back in the day."

"I think he's trouble. If he's sniffing around for Nathan, he'll be back here. We have to do something."

"I'll think on it."

"That's not good enough."

Lawrence held her gaze and his eyes told her that she'd best not challenge him because she was a guppy and he was a shark.

A drunk cowboy staggered up to the bar with a dancing girl guiding him to the spot beside Lawrence.

"Whiskey for me," the cowboy said. "And get the little lady anything she wants."

The girl stepped back, and the bartender reached under the bar and pulled a lever. The floor dropped out from under the cowboy. He didn't even have time to cuss before he fell fifteen feet into a dark holding pen.

The bartender pushed the lever back into place and the trapdoor closed.

The girl smiled at Lawrence. "That's two this evening."

He brushed her away with a nod and a hand gesture.

"She just wants a bit of recognition," Penny said.

"For doing her job? I don't think so."

Penny stared at him a moment, but his eyes were on the men and women in the saloon. Who was drunk or alone? Who could be lured over to the trapdoor without drawing too much attention? The captain was coming in a few days, and Lawrence hadn't met his quota yet. He might have to get a few corpses to build up the numbers, and that meant having someone stuff rats into the sleeves of jackets to make the men seem alive when they were loaded onto the ship.

"Heath, give me another whiskey," Lawrence said to the bartender.

"Yes, sir," Heath said. He filled a glass and slid it over.

Lawrence swirled the amber liquid around in the glass and stared into it, lost in the past, and planning the future. He slammed the drink and set the glass down. The past would always be there, and the future was always in motion. A few bullets here, a few bullets there, and tomorrow's problems could be the next day's triumphs.

Right now he needed more men to sell to the captain. He turned to Penny. "All right, I've thought about it."

"So I should send Rod and Kenneth to kill your old friend?"

Lawrence shook his head. "I said there's no need to kill them. They're worth just as much alive. Tell Rod to work them over good then bring them here. We'll sell them to Captain Andrews this week, and when they heal up, they'll be at sea with nothing to do but work as sailors."

He raised his hand to catch a dancing girl's attention, then pointed toward a lone cowboy entering the bar. A kid in his early twenties who shouldn't have ventured into the neighborhood. Some nights it was almost too easy.

CHAPTER FIVE

Law enforcement tended to avoid
the nine block area called the Barbary
Coast. Life was cheap, and the cut-
throats were as likely to kill lawmen as
anyone else. Jack and Burt stopped by
the sheriff's office, which was less than
a mile away. It was bigger than most,
and two deputies sat at desks drinking
coffee while the sheriff dozed in his
chair. A few lanterns threw light
around the room.

"Howdy," Jack said as he entered.

Burt followed him in and waved to
the men.

"What can we do for you?" one
deputy asked.

"My name is Jack, and this is my
associate, Burt."

"And?"

"Just checking papers," Jack said moving to a board filled with wanted posters.

"Suit yourself."

He flipped through the posters tacked to the board. There were a lot of them. "You men familiar with a man named Lawrence Morton?"

"He and some crazy bitch named Penny run the Redwing."

Jack pulled a poster off the wall showing a sketch of Lawrence with a $500 reward.

"Well, would you look at that," Jack said. "This guy's a mile away and you're passing up on some easy money. What's the story?"

"You don't want to mess with Mr. Morton."

"And evidently you don't either."

"Don't go looking for trouble."

"Not to worry," Jack said. "Trouble always knows where I am. Are any of you familiar with a man named Nathan Townsend?"

The deputy sighed. "Can't say as we are."

"You speak for everyone here?"

"Sometimes."

"Nathan has gone missing."

"Lots of folks go missing."

"I think Lawrence was involved."

"All the more reason for you to not go messing with him."

"Maybe." Jack held up the wanted poster. "In a few days, I'm going to bring Lawrence Morton in here to collect the reward. You might want to make sure you have it ready."

"More likely, you'll end up in a pine box. Lawrence Morton doesn't go anywhere alone."

"Speaking of that," Jack said turning back to the wall of wanted posters. He tugged two more off the wall. "Pretty sure these guys are all on Lawrence's payroll. Get the money for them ready, too. Looks like I'll be doing your job for you and I want to get paid."

"I think you've about worn out your welcome here," the deputy said.

Burt fidgeted. "Maybe we should just go."

The deputy stood. He was almost as tall as Jack. "Your friend is giving you some good advice, stranger. You ought to take it."

Jack grinned. "Are you two on Lawrence's payroll, too?"

"That's a mighty nasty accusation," the other deputy said and stood up, knocking his chair back a few feet.

"Boys," a muffled voice said from beneath a hat. "That'll be enough of that." The sheriff raised one finger and pushed his hat back onto his head.

The deputies backed up, looking sheepish.

The sheriff rose and put a hand on his pistol. "I don't like bounty hunters."

"Most sheriffs don't," Jack said.

"I especially don't like bounty hunters who mouth off to my men."

"No law against that," Jack said.

"Right you are. I tend to be a man of few words, Mr. Coltrane. I'll make an exception here and spell things out for you. Far as I'm concerned, you go into the Redwing or any other saloon and kill a man, whether or not there's a reward offered, I'll arrest you for murder on the spot. Got it?"

"We got it," Burt said. "C'mon, Jack, let's go."

"We'll go when I'm good and ready," Jack said. He stepped up to the sheriff and looked him straight in the eye. "If I find out you or any of your men are on Lawrence Morton's payroll, you'll be hearing from me."

"I look forward to that," the sheriff said. "Get out of my office, and watch your step, Jack Coltrane. We'll be keeping our eyes on you."

Jack grinned. "How many men get murdered every night less than a mile from here? How many more just disappear? There's a reason you let that go on. That reason might be that you're getting paid to stay away, but it might be that you're just afraid to set foot on those streets."

"You'd best get out of here while you can," one of the deputies said.

Jack folded up the wanted posters and tucked them into his pocket. "Not a one of you cowards is fit to wear a badge." He turned and motioned for Burt to go out the door.

"Remember, we're watching you," the sheriff said.

"Watch all you want," Jack said and stepped out into the night.

CHAPTER SIX

Rod and Kenneth were big men with a taste for violence. They strode down the street side by side on their way to give a good beat-down to Jack Coltrane and his friend Burt. Rod grinned as he clenched and unclenched his fists. He couldn't wait to pound in a face or two. He couldn't believe Mr. Morton was willing to pay him for something he'd happily do just for the fun of it. Life was good.

They reached the hotel after midnight. No one tried to stop them when they entered the building and went up the stairs to the second floor. Their victims would likely be sleeping, which made them easy targets. They already knew the room number.

They crept down the hall toward room 207. No light escaped from beneath the door.

"I'm gonna kick the door in," Rod whispered.

Kenneth drew his gun and thumbed back the hammer. He nodded.

Rod felt the adrenaline rush as he reared back and lifted his leg. He kicked the door hard and splintered the jamb. The door swung inward and the two big men rushed into the room.

"Put up your digits!" Kenneth said, pointing his gun at the bed.

The room was empty.

"Damn," Rod said.

"What do we do?" Kenneth asked.

"I guess we wait. Them sumbitches show up, we stomp their heads into the ground."

Kenneth holstered his gun and closed the door, but it drifted open again. He pushed it closed, but with the jamb broken, it creaked and moved inward. "Door won't close."

"Get out of the way," Rod said.

Kenneth moved aside.

Rod pushed the splintered jamb back into place as best he could. He closed the door. The latch wouldn't catch, and the door crept open yet again.

The door to room 209 opened and a big man stepped into the hall. "You boys having trouble?"

"Door's busted," Rod said.

"That tends to happen when you kick it. What's your name?"

"Rod. Why?"

"And you?" the big man asked Kenneth.

"None of your business. Go back to sleep or I'll shoot you in the head."

"I wasn't sleeping, and you're not that good a shot."

"Last warning, asshole," Kenneth said and reached for his gun.

The big man darted forward and punched Kenneth in the nose. Then he reached out and yanked Kenneth's gun from his holster, spun it around, and aimed it at the two men. With his other hand, he reached over and took Rod's gun from his holster, too.

"What the—?" Rod said, eyes wide.

Kenneth cupped his nose and blood trickled between his fingers.

"My name is Jack Coltrane," the man said. "You kicked in the wrong door."

Rod glanced at the number on the door.

"Not your fault," Jack said. "I lied about what room I was in. Back up and take a seat on the bed. Both of you."

Kenneth obeyed. Rod hesitated, but backed up when Jack stepped toward him. Rod sat down beside Kenneth.

The light from the hallway spilled in and lit up their faces. Kenneth's nose was broken. Rod looked irritated. To them, Jack was a large silhouette looming over them.

"Ain't right taking our guns away," Rod said.

"You want your gun back?"

"I know you ain't gonna give it to me. Just ain't right, that's all."

Jack shook his head. He opened the cylinder of Rod's gun, tilted the barrel toward the ceiling and shook the bullets out. They clattered on the floor. He thumbed the cylinder closed and tossed the gun onto the bed beside Rod.

"I'm not a thief," Jack said.

Rod didn't bother to reach for his weapon.

"What about mine?" Kenneth asked, still holding his broken nose.

"I'll give it back to you when I'm done."

"So you ain't gonna kill us?"

"That depends on you. What's your name?"

"None of your business."

Jack couldn't help but grin. "It's easier to shoot someone you don't know. With Rod here I'm thinking maybe he has a mother and father. Maybe he's got a girl on the side who might miss him if I kill him. I see him as more of a living, breathing human being, while you're just a nameless man who'll end up as a statistic. Just another nobody listed as dead in a newspaper, if they bother to count you at all."

"His name is Kenneth," Rod said.

Kenneth glared at Rod.

"We're making progress," Jack said. "I don't normally talk to men like you. I don't normally talk much at all to be honest. I think my buddy, Burt, is rubbing off on me. He talks a lot."

"Where is he?" Rod asked.

"Sleeping down the hall somewhere. He'd be trying to tell me not to kill either of you."

"Burt has the right idea," Rod said.

"Burt doesn't know you're here. If I kill you, I won't tell him. Wouldn't want to worry him, you know."

"Ain't no need to kill us," Rod said.

"Shut up," Kenneth said, his voice pinched and muffled as he held his nose. "He ain't got the stones to kill us."

"Don't need stones," Jack said. "I've got your gun. Bullets work a lot better than stones."

Kenneth glared at him.

"You gonna talk us to death?" Kenneth asked.

"On the trail, Burt kept asking me questions. Kept wanting me to tell him things about myself. Said it's what friends do. They share things. They trust each other. Are you two friends?"

"Yeah," Rod said.

Kenneth rolled his eyes.

"Do you consider Lawrence Morton to be a friend or just an employer?"

"Employer."

"Did either of you ever meet a man named Nathan Townsend?"

Rod hesitated, but nodded.

"Is he dead?"

Another hesitation, then a shrug. "He was alive last I saw him."

"When and where was that?"

"Couple weeks ago. We loaded him with a bunch of other men onto a ship down at the docks. Boss lines up men to crew ships."

"Nathan wasn't a sailor."

"I didn't say the men was all volunteers. Some were, of course, but some don't know they've been recruited. They wake up at sea. That's how it was for Nathan."

"Morton's gonna kill you, Rod," Kenneth said.

Jack grinned. "Shut up, Kenneth, or I might just forget your name."

Kenneth told Jack what he could do with it.

Jack laughed. He liked that Kenneth had enough spunk to talk back considering the circumstances.

Rod explained how things worked. Lawrence was a crimp, a man who forced or trapped men into enlisting as sailors. His favorite method was to throw big parties the night before a ship captain needed a new crew. Pretty dance hall girls would get the men drunk and lead them into temptation with their feminine wiles, then drug the saps. They'd wake up at sea miles from land, so they were forced to work the ship until they reached port somewhere.

"I can't see Nathan falling for that," Jack said.

"Nathan and Lawrence were friends," Rod said. "But Lawrence

wanted Nathan to buy into the saloon. Lawrence owes money to the wrong man, and he's trying to get himself right."

"Who does he owe?"

Rod shrugged. "Above my pay grade."

Jack considered the sheriff's reaction earlier that night. The deputies were touchy about Lawrence, and when Jack pressed it, the sheriff got involved. Was the sheriff controlling things? Maybe Lawrence was working for him. It would explain why the lawmen avoided the Barbary Coast. Of course, getting killed was a good reason to avoid serving warrants, too.

"When does Lawrence have to shanghai a bunch of men again?"

"Hell if I know."

"When is the next big shindig?"

"Tomorrow night."

"So probably the next day for another load of sailors."

Rod shrugged.

Jack emptied Kenneth's gun and tossed it on the bed. "You boys are free to go," he said.

Kenneth stood and glared at Jack. He dropped his empty gun into his holster. Rod did the same, but without all the glaring.

"You and me?" Kenneth said pointing first to Jack and then at himself. "We ain't done."

Jack stepped up close to the man and stared into his eyes. "Good."

"I'm gonna kill you."

"I picked up on the threat the first time," Jack said. He reached up and pinched Kenneth's nose with two fingers. Kenneth yelped, and Jack twisted then let go.

"You son of a bitch!"

"I just set your nose for you, but you might want a doctor to check it. You boys have fun now, you hear?"

CHAPTER SEVEN

The Redwing Saloon operated twenty-four hours a day, but under normal circumstances, Lawrence would have left by one in the morning. These were not normal circumstances. He sat at the bar with a glass of whiskey as girls led men to private rooms upstairs for shows or sex depending on the amount of money exchanged. Lawrence kept thinking about his childhood.

Penny had gone home, which was just as well because her constant nagging was rubbing him wrong. If her father hadn't ponied up most of the money for his part of the saloon, he'd have told her to get the hell out a long time ago. Lawrence hated her father because the man reminded him too much of his own father. When he finally left home, he decided that no man would ever hit him again and live to tell the tale.

He missed Nathan. It was a shame Nathan didn't want to be part of the operation. Lawrence wasn't happy about how things had turned out, but in life, as in poker, you had to play the hand the dealer dealt you. And in life, as in poker, there were those who could cheat and get away with it. Money made a big difference, but it had always been that way and likely always would.

The Redwing brought in plenty of money. Most of it went to the silent partner. The man even had his hands in the crimp side of the business. Lawrence hated being in the position where he had to go along. Overall, the man hadn't been unfair. Lawrence was making more money than he'd ever made. He could take any of the girls upstairs for a roll in the hay as long as he went home to Penny afterward. But he hated having a master. One of these days, he'd find a way to buy the man out or take him down.

Kenneth and Rod entered the Redwing around 1:30 in the morning. Kenneth's nose was messed up, and the men were empty-handed. Lawrence pointed at them until he got their attention, then motioned them over.

The two bruisers approached with hats in hands, staring at the floor.

"Something you want to tell me?"

Lawrence shook his head and refused to speak. Rod tossed a look to his partner, then fixed his eyes on the floorboards.

"We was set up," Rod said.

"Explain."

"We went to room 207 like you said, only it was empty on account of the man was staying in room 209. He caught us by surprise."

"There are two of you."

"Yes, sir," Rod said.

"You were both armed."

"Yes, sir."

"So Jack and his friend Burt stepped into the room behind you and held you at gunpoint?"

"Uh… no sir."

"What happened?"

"It was just the big man."

"Jack."

"Yeah."

"And he held you at gunpoint to tell you something?"

"Yeah, he held us at gunpoint."

"What did he tell you?"

"He was asking about Nathan Townsend."

"And what did you tell him?"

"Nothing. So he broke Kenneth's nose."

"I see."

"So we talked our way out of there and came back here. We just need some more men. That's all."

"There were two of you and one of him. You didn't try to rush him? Didn't distract him so you could draw and shoot him? You didn't do a goddamn thing?"

"Well, Kenneth got his nose broke."

Lawrence turned to Kenneth. "You have anything to add to this nonsensical tale?"

Kenneth shook his head.

Lawrence sighed.

The batwing doors opened and Jack Coltrane stepped into the Redwing all by his lonesome.

"Well, this could get interesting," Lawrence said as Jack nodded to him and started walking his way.

CHAPTER EIGHT

Jack followed Kenneth and Rod back to the Redwing. He waited outside for a few minutes to give them time to go make their report, then he crossed the street and entered the saloon.

The place wasn't as busy as before, but there were still some cowboys at some of the tables, and a few dancing girls sharing drinks with those cowboys in hopes of luring them upstairs for more.

Rod and Kenneth stood in front of Lawrence at the bar. Lawrence's woman, Penny, was nowhere in sight. Jack scanned the crowd. There were two bruisers on the opposite side of the bar from Lawrence. Then there were Kenneth and Rod, if you wanted to count them as bruisers. Jack didn't. Jack caught Lawrence looking at him, so he nodded and crossed the floor to get reacquainted.

"Hello, Lawrence," Jack said as he approached. He nodded to Rod and Kenneth as he stepped up to stand beside them, keeping them between him and the other two bruisers. If those men tried to open fire, they'd hit their own men first. "Howdy, boys. How's the nose?"

"Hurts," Kenneth said.

"Good."

"Welcome back," Lawrence said. "Get you a drink?"

"No thanks," Jack said. "I won't stay long. I just wanted to thank you for the welcoming committee."

Lawrence grinned. "I could have them shoot you right here, right now."

Jack smiled and looked at Kenneth and Rod. "You boys reload your guns yet?"

Rod turned red and Kenneth practically sank into himself.

Lawrence blinked a few times as the question registered. "It would seem my boys might have left a few details out of their report."

Jack laughed. "It happens. I just wanted to stop by to see if I could secure an invitation to your little shindig here tomorrow night."

"You saw the announcement?"

"No, your boys told me about it. Sounds like fun."

"Boys, you can go," Lawrence said.

"Yes, sir," Rod said.

They turned to leave, but Jack put out an arm blocking them. "I'd appreciate it if you'd stick around," he said.

"Why?" Rod asked.

"If I'm being honest, it's so the two men at the bar will have to shoot you before they can shoot me. Buys me a few seconds. You understand."

"You want us to be your shield?"

"Got it in one, Rod," Jack said. "I'm impressed."

"What do you want, Jack?" Lawrence asked.

"I told you. I'm looking for Nathan. Rod here told me about your little operation. Sea captains do need crews."

Lawrence glared at Rod. Then he turned his gaze back to Jack. "That little operation was being run long before I got here."

"Oh, I don't care about that," Jack said. "Men fall for your dirty little tricks, they deserve what they get. Unless one of those men is a friend of mine, that is. Where's Nathan?"

"I don't know."

"Is he alive or dead?"

"Yes."

"Which?"

"He was alive the last time I saw him," Lawrence said. "I hope he's still alive. He's my friend, too, Jack, and I think you know I never had many actual friends."

"Then you shouldn't have sold him to a sea captain."

"This may come as a surprise to you, Jack, but when I asked Nathan to come out here, it was because I'd heard he came into some money, and I thought he'd like to buy a piece of this place."

"I believe you, but I know there's more to the story than that."

"I didn't do anything to Nathan. He walked out of here two, three weeks ago, and he was perfectly fine. I do business, and some of that business might not be completely legal, but I treat my customers right around here."

"That's why you have so many guards to protect you."

Lawrence shook his head. "This is the Barbary Coast, Jack. Dangerous place. A man could step outside and get shot in the back."

"Is that a threat?"

"I would never shoot you in the back. If I shoot you, it will be face to face. And my men aren't under orders to kill you either. I don't want you dead, Jack. Yes, I'd be perfectly happy to sell you to a ship captain. But I have no intention of having you killed. Captains will overlook a few corpses because they know men can die between the time they pass out and the time they wake up. Those men are tossed overboard. But in order to stay in business, I try to make sure the men I supply are still breathing."

"Spoken like a true businessman." Jack nodded. "I'll take that drink now."

Lawrence turned to the bartender. "Heath, two whiskeys."

The glasses slid down the counter and Lawrence caught them. He handed one to Jack, and motioned for Jack to join him at the bar.

Jack moved to sit on the stool beside Lawrence, keeping the man between him and the bruisers at the far end of the bar. "Thanks, Lawrence."

"Rod, Kenneth, pretty sure you can go now," Lawrence said.

"Yes, sir."

"Boys?" Jack said.

The men met his gaze.

"Don't reload until I leave."

They walked away.

Lawrence laughed. "They said you had them at gunpoint."

"I did," Jack said.

Lawrence nodded. "I see. They neglected to mention that you held their own damn guns on them."

Jack shrugged. "Seemed like a good idea at the time."

"You played me."

"No offense, Lawrence, but I don't trust you."

"You have style, Jack. I have to admit that." He held up his whiskey glass.

"To style," Jack said and clinked glasses.

They sipped their drinks.

"What's your story?" Lawrence asked.

"Did a stint in the army, spent a few years as a U.S. Marshal, and now I'm tracking down fugitives."

"Nathan ain't a fugitive," Lawrence said. "He's always been a good man. Ain't sure why he ever liked me, though."

"He must have seen something in you."

Lawrence shook his head. "You never did."

"I never tried."

"You looking to try now?"

Jack shook his head. "Nope. I'm looking to find Nathan, and you know where he is."

"I really don't."

"Do we have to do this dance?"

"Why do you care?" Lawrence asked. "It's not like you were there for Nathan when he needed you."

"What are you talking about?"

Lawrence sighed. "It don't matter. It was a long time ago."

"I haven't heard from Nathan since the war."

"Which war? We fought Indians in the Montana Territory," Lawrence said. "The Battle of the Little Bighorn."

"Custer's Last Stand?" Jack said. "Those men were all killed."

"I guess we were lucky because we were under the command of Major Reno. I'll never forget how we set up in a skirmish line with no idea how large a force we faced. At first, it seemed like we were going to have no real problems. We fired into the village for a good twenty minutes, but then the Indians attacked us. More than five hundred warriors. What a sight. Custer didn't show up. He was supposed to be there with reinforcements. We retreated into the timber by the river, but the Indians set fire to the brush. Nathan pulled me into the water, and we got separated from the other men."

"What happened?"

Lawrence pointed to the scars on his forehead. "Lakota warriors got hold of us when we tried to check our position. Nathan shot at the bastard who tried to scalp me. He missed, but the distraction was all I needed. I broke free and killed that Sioux son of a bitch. Nathan killed the Indian who grabbed him, too. Only the warrior he killed was just a boy. Maybe thirteen years old. I'll never forget the look on his face. Didn't bother me. It was war. You kill or get killed. Anyway, we worked our way back to our men." Lawrence stared at the far wall without seeing anything, lost in the memories. "But ol' Nathan was just never the same. That kid's face haunted him."

Lawrence took a sip of whiskey. He breathed deeply then turned to Jack.

"I hated him for being weak, Jack. That kid would have killed us if he could. He'd have scalped us as he hooted and hollered. Again, you kill or you get killed. Ain't no two ways about it. I was so disgusted that I treated Nathan like last week's garbage until we parted ways. He got out of the army before me. I liked the killing. You like it too. I can see it in your eyes."

"It doesn't bother me," Jack said. "Doesn't mean I like it."

"You keep telling yourself that."

Jack shrugged and sipped his whiskey. "I will."

"I didn't hear from Nathan for a few years. He'd gone back to spend time with his folks in Springfield before they moved out here. I always liked his mama, but his pops sure hated me. Guess it was all the short jokes."

"Right."

"I ain't kidding myself, Jack. Ol' Tuck said I had the darkness in me. I never knew what that meant until I joined the army and started killing Indians. But I only killed enemies. And I ain't killed no one who didn't deserve it since I left the army."

Jack pulled the wanted posters out of his pocket. He unfolded them and put Lawrence's on top. "This tells another story."

"That was self-defense. Them boys drew first." Lawrence laughed. "Wait a minute. You ain't really here about Nathan, are you? You just want to take me in for the reward."

"The reward is just a bonus," Jack said. "I'm going to find out what really happened to Nathan, then I'm taking you," Jack moved Lawrence's poster to the bottom, "this man," he pointed to the poster then at one of the men at the end of the bar. He moved that poster to the bottom, pointed to the picture on the top then at the other man at the bar, "and this man in to collect my pay,"

"Just like that."

Jack nodded.

"And you don't mind telling me this."

"Won't change anything. You're going to tell me what really happened to Nathan. I don't think it's your fault. You were either following orders or it happened without your knowledge."

"Following orders? Jesus, how much did Rod tell you?"

"Enough."

Lawrence shook his head. "Truth be told, I wanted Nathan to buy out my share of the Redwing. The silent partner is more trouble than he's worth."

"What's his name?" Jack asked.

Again, Lawrence gave him a head shake. "That's not how this works, Jack."

"How does it work, Lawrence?"

"First, you need to lose that poster of me."

"They'll have more up at the sheriff's office."

"The law doesn't get enforced in this neighborhood. I'll tell you what I know, but in exchange, you gotta kill the son of a bitch, and you can't turn me in."

"I'm going to figure it out anyway," Jack said.

"Sure you will. Immunity for me and I'll talk."

"Not for your men?"

"I don't give a good goddamn what happens to them. Their type is as common as the whores we hire in here. I can replace them before you drag them down to collect your cash."

"They're not worth much."

"True, but if I don't share the secret, you'll be killed before you know the real score. So the question you gotta ask yourself is, how much is it worth to you to find out what really happened to Nathan?"

"I'm not going to kill anyone for you, Lawrence."

"My silent partner will be here tomorrow night. He rarely comes in, but I told him I might need his help because you're snooping around. My guess is he'll try to have you killed, which is why you'll be willing to shoot him."

Jack finished his drink. "Have I told you that I don't like you?"

"Only every time you see me."

"Don't want you to forget that."

"I won't."

Jack sighed.

"I'm a pain in the ass," Lawrence said. "But I have to look out for my own best interests." Lawrence patted Jack on the shoulder. "You think it over. Come back tomorrow night, Jack. I guarantee you won't be bored."

CHAPTER NINE

The actual hotel where Jack and Burt were staying wasn't in the section known as the Barbary Coast. Instead, it sat a bit inland. The price was steep, but Jack didn't want to lay his head down in the most dangerous part of town. His senses would be in constant heightened awareness. Far better to relax in comfort. Danger would still snap him awake.

The next morning, Jack and Burt left their rooms and went down for breakfast. As they walked toward the dining hall, a plain-looking woman in a long black dress entered the hotel and approached the desk. Another woman blocked the door to the dining hall as she argued with the wait staff.

"What kind of nonsense is this?" she demanded.

The waiter looked at Jack apologetically. "I'll be right with you, sir," he said.

Jack nodded and glanced over to the desk where the woman in black spoke to the clerk. Jack overheard part of her conversation.

"...Looking for my brother. He's been missing for two weeks, and I was hoping maybe he stayed here."

"What was his name?" the clerk asked.

"Russell Sands."

"I'll check our guest book."

"Thank you. I'm just so worried. It's not like him to just disappear like this."

"I don't see a Russell Sands in the log, Mrs. Parker."

"Call me Martha," she said.

"Doesn't alter the facts, Mrs... Sorry. Martha."

Jack's attention went back to the arguing woman. She huffed and stormed away, knocking Burt aside as she went.

Jack looked back at Martha.

"Are you familiar with the saloons in town?" Martha asked the clerk. "I'm looking for a place called the Redwing."

Jack started to turn toward her, but the waiter cleared his throat. "Sorry to keep you waiting, sir. Table for two?"

"My brother had a business offer from the owner," Martha said.

"That's right," Burt said. "Jack?"

"Sorry," Jack said. "I was distracted." He looked back to see Martha thanking the clerk and turning to leave.

"You coming?" Burt asked.

Jack hesitated a moment, then turned to Burt. "Get us a table," he said. "I'll join you in a minute. I want to talk to that woman."

Burt glanced at Martha. He shrugged, and tailed the waiter into the dining area.

Jack followed Martha toward the front door. "Excuse me, ma'am," Jack said, taking off his hat.

Martha turned to face him. "Are you talking to me?"

"Yes, ma'am," Jack said, holding his hat at his waist.

"I don't know you."

"I couldn't help but overhear your conversation," Jack said.

"Did you know my brother?"

Jack shook his head. "No, but I know the Redwing."

"Can you give me directions?"

"No offense, ma'am, but it's not the kind of place you should visit."

"I have to find my brother."

"Maybe I can help with that. Can I buy you breakfast? We can talk about it."

She hesitated. "I don't normally dine with strangers."

"My name is Jack Coltrane."

"Martha Parker."

"My wife was named Martha," Jack said.

"Was?"

Jack nodded.

"Then we can't be strangers anymore."

Jack led her into the dining area. They joined Burt at a table toward the back. Half the tables were occupied, while others needed to be cleared as dirty dishes sat atop them.

"Martha, meet Burt," Jack said. "Burt, this is Martha. Her brother, Russell Sands, went missing after going to the Redwing two weeks ago."

"Sorry to hear that," Burt said and nodded toward Jack. "His friend went missing there, too."

"Really?"

Jack nodded. "Afraid so."

The waiter stopped by to take their orders then left them.

"The Redwing is a dangerous place," Jack said. "You can tell me about Russell, and I'll see if I can find out what happened to him."

She narrowed her eyes. "I think you have suspicions."

"I do."

"Care to share them?"

"The minority holder of the Redwing offered my friend the opportunity to buy in."

"Minority holder?"

"Near as I can tell, the saloon is owned by two men. Lawrence Morton holds part of the deed, and the rest—"

"Lawrence Morton? That's the man Russell was going to see. They were in the army together. Seventh Cavalry Regiment."

"I'm sensing a pattern," Jack said.

"Your friend was in the same regiment?"

"Nathan Townsend."

"Small world. Russell and Nathan were friends and business partners. They found gold in the hills, and staked a claim."

Jack considered this. Had Russell and Nathan gone to see Lawrence together? Lawrence hadn't mentioned it, but that would only complicate things.

"I need to find Russell," Martha said. "Our mother is sick and the doctor says she doesn't have much time. He should be there for her."

"I don't think that's going to happen."

"Why not? She's just down in Silver Mountain City. It's a few days ride. Wait. Don't tell me you think he's dead!"

The waiter returned with plates of eggs and bacon. Martha got herself under control.

"Your meals," the waiter said. "Is there anything else I can get you?"

"No thanks," Burt said.

The waiter tossed a concerned look at Martha as he walked away.

"I think Russell is alive, but it may be months before he can get back here."

"Why?"

"Because I think he's probably been shanghaied on a ship. I think the same thing happened to Nathan, but I'm working to verify that. I want to be sure."

"Will you please find out about my brother? I have to head back to Silver Mountain City the day after tomorrow."

"I'll have news for you before then."

She placed a hand on Jack's hand. "Thank you."

Jack gave her a nod.

"No, really. Thank you." Tears welled in her eyes.

Women always had to be so emotional, Jack thought. It made him uncomfortable. "It's all right," he said and patted her hand.

CHAPTER TEN

Later that morning, Martha entered the General Store. She went down an aisle, looking at merchandise. A few minutes later, a sheriff's deputy approached her. "He'll see you now," the deputy said.

"Lead the way," Martha said.

The deputy led her behind the counter of the store. The owner looked at them, but did not object. They went into the back room, and into a small office.

"Did he take the bait?" her employer asked.

She nodded. "He did. I may have oversold it a bit."

"Did you tell him your name was Martha?"

"Yes, I did everything just like you said."

"Excellent. Not to worry, my dear. You just make sure you're at the saloon tonight. I may need you as a distraction."

"Are you going to kill Jack?"

"If I wanted him dead, would I go to this much trouble?"

"So why *are* you going to so much trouble?"

He gave her a head shake. "I'm paying you well enough to not ask me such questions. Besides, I'm not much for talking."

"It just seems overly complicated."

He sighed. "It wasn't supposed to be."

CHAPTER ELEVEN

When Jack and Burt entered the saloon that night, the place was already standing room only. The music was loud. The women were dancing. The men were drinking.

They squeezed past a throng of men crowding the dance floor for the best view of a lovely young woman who kept flashing her goods at them. The men practically drooled on themselves as they reached toward her. One of the men Jack planned to collect a reward on stood on the side of the dance floor and kept swatting hands away from the woman.

When Jack finally made it to an open area, a man stepped up to him holding a baseball bat. "Fifty cents, and you can take a swing at me."

Jack stared at the man. "Why would I want to do that?"

"For fun."

Jack pushed past him.

The man stepped into Burt's path. "How about you, sir?"

"What's your name?" Burt asked.

"My name is Leonard, but folks call me Oofty Goofty. Fifty cents and you can hit me with the bat. What do you say?"

"What the hell kinda name is Oofty Goofty?"

"Do you want to take a swing or don't you?"

Burt held up fifty cents. "I don't want to take a swing, but I want to know about the name."

The man snatched the coins and pocketed them. He leaned close to Burt. "I used to do an act where I was known as the Wild Man of Borneo. I used tar and yak fur to make myself look like something you'd see in a jungle, and I made funny sounds. Oofty Goofty was one of them, and it just kinda stuck."

Burt shook his head and tried to spot Jack, but he lost him in the crowd. "Damn."

A dancing girl slid up close to Burt. "Hey, cowboy," she said. "Remember me?"

Burt grinned. She was the ginger willing to do anything. "I do."

"Want to come up to my room?"

Burt looked in the direction Jack had gone, but the crush of bodies was too much. He couldn't see Jack anywhere. He had money, and the woman was gorgeous, and Jack could take care of himself. "I sure do," Burt said.

The woman took his hand and pulled him across the dance floor to the stairs. Burt's smile stretched from ear to ear, and the front of his trousers stretched a bit too. "You're on your own, Jack," he whispered. "It's time for a slice of heaven."

Meanwhile, Jack worked his way to the bar. A few men stood on the trapdoor, and while Jack hadn't seen it in action, he recognized it for what it was because Lawrence put too much effort into trying to get him to stand there.

Penny leaned against the bar beside Lawrence, who remained ever vigilant on the crowd.

Jack didn't approach them. He kept himself hidden from view in the throngs of noisy people. As he always did upon entering a crowded room, he scanned the place for exits. He looked for anyone paying him too much attention. He also looked for anyone who appeared dangerous, though in this place that meant damn near everyone. So he limited himself to those who either clicked things up a notch, or those who appeared too calm for the situation.

Most of the men were having fun. They were talking to friends. They were gawking at half naked women. They were drinking.

A few people observed the room around them. Most of those were the bruisers Lawrence hired as security. One group was different from the others. They had a corner table, and Jack watched them through the gaps in the crowd. It took him a moment to recognize them. The sheriff and his deputies.

That wasn't good.

He couldn't tell whether or not they were drinking. Were they on duty? Were they wearing badges? Were they here for extra security? The sheriff would like nothing more than to arrest a bounty hunter should things go south tonight. Then again, the way the sheriff had talked before, and what Martha had said made him wonder if perhaps the sheriff was the majority holder in the Redwing. It made sense. He and his deputies never tried to bring Lawrence in, but here they were in the saloon. Even if the sheriff wasn't the silent partner, he could still be on the take.

He'd have to watch his step.

The other bruisers were easy to spot. Lawrence had hired a few extras to handle the crowd. There were a few who could be on the payroll, but they might just be wary in a room full of drunk cowboys and sailors. An attractive woman slipped up next to Jack. She wore more clothes than the dancing girls, and she held a leather bound book.

She said something to him, but he couldn't hear her so he leaned closer and cupped his hand to his ear.

"You're a strapping man," she said.

"You're a fine looking woman," he said.

"I'm recruiting sailors for Captain Andrews. Ship leaves the docks tomorrow morning."

"Do I look like a sailor to you?"

She smiled. "You look like you can do anything you set your mind to."

"No thanks."

She shrugged. "Have a nice night." She moved to the next man and repeated the procedure.

Jack waited until she was finished then tapped her on the shoulder. She turned. "Changed your mind, cowboy?"

"No. Who has you recruiting here tonight?"

"Mr. Morton, of course. We always recruit on party nights."

Jack nodded. He realized that Lawrence lined up as many legitimate recruits as possible then filled the quota with the men his people got drunk or drugged. So at least part of the operation was above board. Good to know.

He still didn't like Lawrence that much.

And he was still going to take him in for the reward as soon as he verified what happened to Nathan.

Jack spotted an open stool next to Lawrence. It was just to the side of the trapdoor.

No reason not to join him.

Jack slipped through the people to come up on Lawrence from an unexpected direction, but as soon as he slid onto the seat, Lawrence said, "I saw you when you came in, Jack."

"I wasn't hiding."

"I still don't have anything to tell you about Nathan."

"I figured as much. Have you heard of a man named Russell Sands?"

"Was he that runt in school who used to pick his nose and eat it all the damn time?"

"No."

"Hmm. Name sounds vaguely familiar, but I can't place it. Who is he?"

"Guy you took a meeting with about buying into the business here."

Lawrence nodded. "That's right. We were both in the Seventh Cavalry. He was friends with Nathan, not me, but yeah, I offered to sell him my stake in the Redwing a few weeks back, but he didn't have any money."

"But you have trouble remembering him?"

"Jack, I've taken a lot of meetings in the past month. Truth be told, I'm sick of this place. I'd happily sell to you if you were interested."

"Pass."

Lawrence turned and waved his hand at the bartender. "Heath, two whiskeys."

As always, the bartender filled the glasses and slid them down, but in the din, it was impossible to hear them glide along the wooden counter. Lawrence handed Jack a drink.

"Last of the free drinks for you, Jack. From now on, you'll have to buy your own."

Jack turned around to face the mirror along the bar. He didn't like having his back exposed to the space behind the bar. He could watch the room in the mirror. It wasn't optimal, but he had a feeling someone was watching him, and he always trusted his gut.

"No problem," Jack said.

Lawrence leaned back and grinned. "It's gonna be a fun night. I can feel it."

"Don't get too comfortable."

"Why not?"

"Because before the night is over, I'm going to take you and your boys in to collect the reward."

Lawrence laughed. "You don't really expect us to cooperate on that front."

Jack grinned and lifted his glass. "I certainly hope not."

And so it went.

CHAPTER TWELVE

The crowd thinned over the next few hours as people went home or ventured upstairs with the dancing girls. The men who went with the girls never seemed to come down. Some men passed out at their tables, and the bruisers quietly moved them to the back room.

Jack paid for a few drinks. Lawrence occasionally chatted with him, but mostly talked to Penny, directing her to keep the girls busy. Jack realized he hadn't seen Burt in a while, but he wasn't concerned. The strange guy with the baseball bat wandered in and out of the saloon. Jack watched him enter again with a sailor. He was clearly giving his spiel, and the sailor kept shaking his head. As they separated, Jack saw a familiar face enter the Redwing. Tuck the dwarf.

A few girls took to the floor to lure drunks with hints of the pleasures they could find, and Jack lost sight of Tuck.

What was he doing here?

Jack slipped away from the bar and maneuvered his way across the floor. When he reached the other side of the room, he spotted Tuck standing in front of the table where the sheriff and his deputies sat.

"Howdy, Sheriff," Jack said with a nod. "Deputies."

They nodded back, but didn't speak.

"What brings you out here, Tuck?" Jack asked.

Tuck turned and looked up at him. He pulled a pencil and a sheet of foolscap paper from his pocket and jotted a note that read, *Looking for Nathan.*

Jack shook his head. "I'm handling that. I'll have more information tomorrow."

"What's with the paper?" one of the deputies asked. "Why ain't you talking?"

"He's soft-spoken," Jack said. "Hard to raise his voice enough to be heard in here."

The deputy chuckled.

"You think that's funny?" Jack asked.

"He always struck me as the mouthy type," the deputy said.

Jack frowned and narrowed his gaze. He didn't like bullies.

Tuck held up a hand and shook his head. Jotted, *Let it go* on the page.

"Let me buy you a drink, Tuck," Jack said.

Tuck shook his head.

"I insist," Jack said. "You're here, you can use a whiskey."

"Might help his vocal cords," the deputy said and laughed.

"You're not funny," Jack said.

"We think he's funny," the other deputy said pointing to the sheriff and himself.

The sheriff frowned. "That's enough, boys."

"This way, Tuck," Jack said and guided him toward the bar.

Tuck sighed and walked with him. Lawrence and Penny were locked up in a disagreement about something and didn't look at them.

But Heath, the bartender, spotted them as they approached. "The usual, sir?" Heath said.

Tuck nodded.

"You come in here enough to have a usual?" Jack asked.

Tuck shrugged.

Lawrence turned as Tuck pushed himself up on the barstool. "Howdy, Tuck," he said.

Tuck gave him a nod.

Lawrence looked at Jack. Something was off about the way he studied him. Jack glanced at the floor to make sure he wasn't standing on the trapdoor. He was fine.

"Something wrong, Lawrence?"

"Not at all," Lawrence said.

Tuck looked at Jack and patted the bar beside him.

"I'm fine where I am," Jack said, reaching over to grab his whiskey.

Tuck spun around to use the counter as a base so he could write out another note. He held it up to Jack. *Any progress to report?*

"Not yet."

Tuck jotted another note that read, *Tired of waiting.*

"Me too," Jack said.

"What are you two yammering about?" Lawrence asked and snatched the paper. He turned it so Penny could read it.

She nodded and wandered away toward the front of the saloon.

Jack grabbed the paper back and returned it to Tuck. "Don't let him push you around," Jack said.

Tuck grinned.

"I'm not pushing him around," Lawrence said.

"Maybe you and I should step outside so I can teach you some manners."

"Calm down, Jack. Tuck don't mind."

Tuck shrugged and shook his head.

"See?" Lawrence said.

Jack's patience was about used up. "Show some respect."

"I've got nothing but respect for ol' Tuck," Lawrence said.

Tuck pushed Lawrence's arm then gave a quick head shake.

Jack wasn't sure what that was all about, but he didn't get the chance to ask because a familiar voice called his name. He spun around to see Martha standing on the dance floor with a torn dress and a shattered look on her face.

"Jack!" she said, tears streaming down her face.

"What's wrong, Martha?"

"Russell is dead."

She rushed into his arms.

Jack held her for a moment. "I'm sorry to hear that," he said. "What happened?"

She looked up at him. "This," she said, and shoved him backward as hard as she could.

Jack wasn't expecting it, so he stepped back.

The floor gave way beneath him.

Jack fell, but managed to catch the edge of the floor with his fingers. He dangled in the air a good fifteen feet from a hard rocky floor. He grunted and tried to pull himself back up.

"I did good?" Martha asked.

"You did good," Tuck said. "Allow me to finish."

The dwarf jumped off his stool and stomped hard on Jack's fingers. Jack lost his grip and fell.

CHAPTER THIRTEEN

Jack hit the ground hard. The trapdoor slammed closed above him and he found himself in darkness. A thin outline of light stretched out in a rectangle above him where the trapdoor didn't quite match up to the floor.

He pulled his gun and considered firing through the floor, but he couldn't tell where anyone was, so it would be a waste of bullets.

He shook his head and let the truth sink in.

Martha had turned to Tuck and he had responded.

Jack knew Tuck could speak, of course, but he so rarely bothered and the words had never been so loud and clear, and each was a punch to the gut.

After a time, Jack's eyes adjusted to the darkness. He holstered his gun and checked out his surroundings. He stood in a large cage. He was alone. A terrible smell permeated the air. Death. He'd smelled it before on battlefields and on the trail after coming upon travelers massacred by bandits.

A door led to another room, but that door was closed. Another opening on the wall to his left led to stairs heading up to the saloon. A table stood in one corner. It was piled high with something, but in the darkness, it was impossible to determine the contents.

Jack found the door to the cage, but it was locked with a padlock. He tried pulling on the lock, but it wouldn't budge. He could slip his hands through the bars, but couldn't reach far because his forearms were too large. He pulled his hands back in. The bars plunged into the dirt floor. The top of the cage had a mere inch of clearance, and tall as he was, he couldn't reach the top.

There seemed to be no way out.

But Jack was not the kind of man to sit down and wait. Any minute someone could come down those stairs and simply shoot him where he stood. He had his guns. There was no reason to hesitate, so now that he could see well enough, he drew his gun, slipped it through the bars, and while it wasn't easy to get a good aim at such an awkward angle, he had to try.

He aimed at the padlock and pulled the trigger.

The first bullet struck the body of the padlock, and did some damage, but the lock held. The second bullet struck the shackle. It shattered. Jack pulled the lock from the door. He pushed the door open and stepped out of the cage.

If anyone above heard the shots, they might come down. Would they come down those stairs or was there another staircase behind the closed door.

Jack checked the door first.

It was locked.

A good kick took care of that.

He put his shoulder into it and broke through the door. Twenty men dozed on the floor in the large room. Most were drunks who had passed out. A few had been drugged. Three were dead, and at least one of the corpses had been there long enough to start smelling.

One of the drugged men was Burt.

None of them were going to be of any assistance, so Jack left them there. He went back into the cage room and checked the staircase.

No one had come down.

Had they not heard the shots?

He crept up the steps. They creaked a bit, and he knew the noise could be louder than he realized because his ears were still ringing from the shots he'd fired. Regardless, the creaking steps weren't loud enough to be heard over the noise inside the saloon, and as Jack reached the door, he could hear the party still going on out there.

The door wasn't locked. He pulled it open and stepped into the back room of the saloon.

The room was stacked with crates of whiskey. A desk with an open ledger sat in the center of the room, with a wooden chair pushed back.

Jack grinned. He approached the door to the saloon, eased it open. It led directly to the backside of the bar, and he watched Heath pouring glasses of whiskey for customers.

Jack stepped into sight, but Lawrence and Tuck had their backs to him as they surveyed the customers. Martha was nowhere in sight, though Penny still had her usual position beside Lawrence.

A drunk sailor spotted Jack and tilted his head slightly.

Jack put a finger to his lips.

The sailor grinned and nodded, then turned toward Heath who slid him a drink.

The bruisers were watching the customers. Jack could have taken Heath's place pouring drinks and no one would have noticed.

This amused him.

Normally, the people dropped through the trapdoor were drunk and a fall like that would leave them dazed and confused. Lawrence had underestimated Jack, and that was going to be his downfall. But Heath had pulled the lever that sent Jack plummeting into the cage. Turnabout was fair play.

Jack dropped his gun back into his holster. He stepped up to the bar, reached down and pulled the lever.

Tuck heard the door open and turned.

Heath caught Jack in his peripheral vision.

Jack reached out and grabbed him.

"Say goodnight," Jack said and hurled him over the bar. Heath dropped through the trapdoor.

Tuck tried to get up, but Jack jumped onto the counter, kicked Tuck hard in the head toward the trapdoor. Tuck tumbled off his stool, hit the edge of the door and dropped into the cage. The cage was no longer locked, but it was a good drop so Jack didn't need to worry about him coming up the stairs until he recovered.

Lawrence turned. Jack slid off the edge of the bar onto the stool Tuck had occupied. Jack threw an arm around Lawrence's neck and pulled him close.

"You shanghaied Nathan, didn't you?"

"Men!" Lawrence yelled.

One of the bruisers saw Jack manhandling Lawrence. The bruiser drew his gun.

Jack was faster.

Jack fired.

So did the bruiser.

The bruiser missed.

Jack did not.

The bruiser stumbled back a step with a hole in his forehead. He staggered another two steps, then collapsed.

Jack smacked Lawrence on the head with the butt of his gun, dazing him.

"You shanghaied Nathan, didn't you?" he repeated.

Lawrence blinked.

Penny darted into the crowd. Jack didn't care about her so much. With the sound of the gunshots, a few people hit the deck, but most rushed for the exit. With a few notable exceptions. The sheriff and his deputies.

"It was you, right, Lawrence?"

Lawrence shook his head. "Tuck runs the show," he said, his voice wonky. "I only follow orders."

The sheriff and the deputies aimed their guns at Jack.

But Jack held Lawrence in front of him.

"You shot that man," the sheriff said. "Put your gun down, Coltrane. You're under arrest."

"That was self-defense."

"We don't care."

"You will."

Jack shoved Lawrence forward.

Lawrence, still dazed staggered toward the sheriff.

Jack did a shoulder roll behind Lawrence, but at an angle. One of the deputies fired. The other deputy and the sheriff didn't have a shot as they had to catch Lawrence. The deputy's shot missed. Jack came to his feet beside the deputy. He hammered his fist into the deputy's face. The deputy dropped like a stone.

Jack rushed the other deputy, who panicked. Jack slammed into him, driving him into the sheriff. Both men careened into the wall beside a befuddled Oofty Goofty, who held his baseball bat in one hand staring wide-eyed at the sheriff and deputy all elbows and knees locked up as they tumbled to the ground.

"Can I borrow your bat?" Jack asked.

Oofty handed it to him. "Uh, sure?"

Jack grabbed the bat, spun around and threw it across the room. The bat flipped end over end and this time his aim was perfect. It smacked the other bruiser in the face. The man hit the floor hard and his gun skittered away.

"Nice throw," Oofty said.

"Practice makes perfect," Jack said.

The rest of the customers, who weren't hiding under tables or passed out in a booth, pushed through the front door to escape the saloon.

Jack took the sheriff's gun and kicked the deputy's pistol away.

Then he walked over and punched Lawrence in the nose.

"That's for not helping your friend."

Lawrence sat down and cupped his face.

The sheriff disentangled himself from his deputy. He started to speak, but Jack pointed the sheriff's own gun at him.

"Are you involved in all this?" Jack asked.

"All what?"

"The business of the saloon for one. The capturing of men and selling them to ship captains for another."

"I'm the damn sheriff!"

"Are you taking bribes on the side to look away? Maybe to help keep the peace on party nights when men are being lured away by pretty women who drug them or by the bruisers who grab the drunks?"

Tuck burst through the door behind the bar. He climbed up onto the counter, but Jack saw him as he struggled to get into position.

"That's far enough, Tuck," Jack said, aiming a gun at him and another at the sheriff.

Tuck had a gun in one hand. Blood ran from his nose, and he favored one leg as he tried to crawl down from the bar onto one of the stools.

"Drop the gun, Tuck."

The dwarf sighed and placed the gun on the bar.

"Push it away."

Tuck pushed it down the counter.

"Sorry, Jack," Tuck said.

"What the hell happened?"

"Lawrence wanted out. I needed someone I trusted to run the business.

I met one of Nathan's friends from the army, and he refused us."

"Russell Sands?"

Tuck nodded.

Jack narrowed his eyes. "What about his sister?"

Tuck laughed and wiped blood from his face. "So far as I know, he doesn't have a sister. You met one of our dancing girls. I told her to use the name Martha to distract you."

"Hate to interrupt," Oofty Goofty said, and pointed.

The bruiser Jack had smacked with the bat tried to get up, but he couldn't find his balance.

"We'll get back to this in a minute," Jack said. He turned to the sheriff and nodded to the bruiser struggling with a concussion. "Sheriff, cuff that man. He's wanted for murder. Dead guy on the floor over there was also wanted for murder. And of course, my old friend Lawrence too."

Sheriff kept his hands up as he crossed the floor because Jack held a gun on him the entire time. The deputy moved to a seated position and held his face and winced when he tried to move his arm. The sheriff cuffed the bruiser.

"I wasn't involved in all this," the sheriff said.

"Yes you were," Jack said. "But that's not my problem. You're going to wire for my money, you're going to sign off on the dead guy having drawn first, and you're not going to run for re-election."

"Money, yes," the sheriff said. "Dead guy, self-defense. But you don't live here, so you can't stop me from running."

Jack laughed. "You're right. And that's fine, but you need to arrest Tuck here for his illegal operations."

"He won't do that," Tuck said. "I've paid him well."

"Tuck, you're under arrest for kidnapping, illegal gambling, and murder," the sheriff said as he cuffed the bruiser.

"I didn't kill anyone."

"Courts can decide that."

"I'll take you down with me."

The sheriff sighed. "We'll see."

Jack crossed the floor and stared down at Tuck. "What the hell happened to you, Tuck? You were a good man. Did you kill Nathan?"

Tuck shook his head. "I would never kill my own son, Jack. Jesus! You know me better than that."

"I thought I did."

"Mabel and I had nothing when we moved out here. Lawrence had part of the saloon here. When the owner got sick, Mabel took care of him and he gifted the saloon to me, but I never told Mabel because she wouldn't approve of the crimping operations. But that's the bulk of the money coming in here. So Lawrence and I ran it. Lawrence wanted out. He thought Nathan would take over, but Nathan was disgusted. He was going to tell Mabel."

"So you dropped him through the trapdoor and sold him to a sea captain."

Tuck nodded. "But he's still alive."

"So far as you know. Anything can happen at sea."

"Hell, anything can happen here. You just single-handedly took down my entire operation."

"Why even call me out here?"

"I didn't! Mabel found out Nathan went missing. She doesn't know I'm the silent partner here, but she knew Lawrence had a price on his head so she sent for you. I thought you'd give up sooner and just take the damn reward for Lawrence. Wishful thinking."

"Nathan was my friend."

"But you're a bounty hunter."

Jack shook his head. "And you sent Martha? Why?"

"To make sure you were here tonight. Your friend was easy enough to lure away." Tuck sighed. "Things just got all out of hand. You're going to tell Mabel."

"You're damn right I am."

"She'll never forgive me."

"Good," Jack said. "I hope you never forgive yourself either."

"What now?" the sheriff asked.

Jack looked at the man, disgusted. "Now you do your damn job."

CHAPTER FOURTEEN

A spider crawled across the counter at the Cobweb Palace. Jack slid a peanut down to the parrot who eagerly snatched and ate it. Burt sat on a stool looking out of sorts.

Mabel entered the bar and walked over. "The sheriff filled me in," she said. "According to the ledger, Nathan is on a ship called the Santiago. It should dock in Spain next month. I'm sending a message to him to be delivered there so he can come home."

"Sorry about Tuck."

She stared at the floor. "Me too. I should have known. He wasn't the same after Nathan disappeared, and I mistook his emotions for worry about Nathan rather than worry that I'd find out he was responsible. How can you spend your entire life with someone and still not know them?"

"How can you ever really expect to know anyone?" Jack asked.

Mabel looked into his eyes. She was a strong woman and she would be all right. She put a hand on Jack's shoulder. "I know you," she said. "You're always stalwart and true, and you always do the right thing if you can find it."

Jack pulled her into an embrace. "If you need anything," he said.

"I know how to reach you," she said. "Thank you for everything. Thank you for finding out about Nathan. Thank you for getting to the truth about Tuck. And thank you for always being a good man."

"I learned the importance of that from you, Mabel."

"It didn't rub off on Tuck."

"Maybe not, but he initially did what he did for you. And your influence certainly held true with Nathan."

She smiled. "And with a little luck, I'll see him again before too long."

Jack nodded. "You will."

"We should get moving," Burt said. "Money should be at the sheriff's office by now."

"We'll pick it up on our way out of town," Jack said.

"You be safe," Mabel said.

Jack grinned. "No fun in that."

Mabel shook her head and motioned to Abe, who stood at the end of the bar in his big black top hat. "Hot toddy?" she said.

"Coming right up," Abe said.

Jack and Burt walked toward the exit of the Cobweb Palace. "How you feeling, Burt?"

"Stupid," Burt said. "I thought that dancing girl liked me."

"Really?"

"Well, I thought she liked my money."

"She did like your money. Hell, she got all your money."

"And all I got was a big, steaming helping of embarrassment."

"Chew it slowly and swallow it, Burt. You live and learn or you don't live long."

And the batwing doors swung closed behind them.

Made in the USA
Monee, IL
21 June 2020

34258527R00083